6/15/15

3 9082 12969 4215

D1563994

Bridget Gadget

Techie
Cheater

written by Mari Kesselring
illustrated by Mariano Epelbaum

12 STORY LIBRARY

www.12StoryLibrary.com

12-Story Library is an imprint of Peterson Publishing Company and Press Room Editions.

Produced for 12-Story Library by Red Line Editorial

Illustrations by Mariano Epelbaum

ISBN
978-1-63235-038-1 (hardcover)
978-1-63235-098-5 (paperback)
978-1-62143-079-7 (hosted ebook)

Library of Congress Control Number: 2014937410

Printed in the United States of America
Mankato, MN
June, 2014

Table of Contents

Chapter 1   A New View   5

Chapter 2   Desperation   14

Chapter 3   Making a Deal   18

Chapter 4   Top Secret Test   25

Chapter 5   A Liar and a Cheat   31

Chapter 6   No Other Choice   36

Chapter 7   Agent Gadget   42

Chapter 8   Undercover   47

Chapter 9   Coming Clean   52

Think About It   60

Write About It   61

About the Author   62

About the Illustrator   63

More Fun with Bridget Gadget   64

1

A New View

"Happy Birthday!" Bridget's dad
smiled as he handed her a small,
brightly wrapped package.

Bridget knew immediately that her dad
hadn't done the wrapping himself. It was way
too neat. Her dad, Nick Grant, owned Lingo,
a big technology company in Cyber Hills.
He was great at developing cool new gadgets.
But simple things like wrapping a present or
kicking around a soccer ball always baffled
him. His assistant Lisa had probably wrapped
her present.

At least Bridget was pretty sure her dad
had picked out the gift himself. He was good
at that. Her dad usually gave her cutting-edge
tech products for her birthday. She loved
gadgets so much that most of her friends
called her Bridget Gadget.

Bridget's hands shook with excitement as she untied the bow and ripped through the wrapping paper. She couldn't wait to see what new gadget her dad had given her.

She lifted the lid on a small box.

"Oh . . . wow." Bridget's voice faltered as she stared inside the box. Carefully wrapped in tissue paper was a pair of wide-rimmed, plastic-framed glasses. Bridget didn't even wear glasses.

"Glasses?" she said finally, lifting them out of the box.

Bridget's dad chuckled.

"Very special glasses," he said with a smile. "Put them on."

Bridget slipped the lightweight frames on and peered through the lenses.

"Everything looks the same," she said, scanning the living room. She caught her own reflection in the mirror by the fireplace. The glasses looked really good on her. They made her look smarter and older. But there had to be more to them than that, she thought. Then she noticed that her dad was typing something on his smartphone.

Seconds later the words *Happy Birthday, Bridg*! appeared on the right lens of the glasses.

"Wow!" Bridget exclaimed.

"Pretty cool, huh?" He dad smiled. "They're synced up to your smartphone. So the glasses show text messages right on the lenses. We're calling them YouViews—a brand new Lingo product. You can't even buy them in stores until their official release next month."

Bridget jumped off the couch and gave her dad a giant hug.

"Thanks! They're so cool."

"YouViews can also track where you're looking," her dad explained. "You can make videos and take pictures just by looking at something and giving a command."

"Really? I couldn't even tell they had a camera."

"It's hidden in the frame," her dad explained.

Bridget looked directly at her dad and said, "Take picture." The picture she'd just taken of her dad appeared on the right lens.

"That's amazing!" Bridget breathed.

"I'm glad you like them," he said. "But there is one rule about this gadget . . ."

Bridget sighed, plopping back down on the couch. Her dad had rules about everything.

"No one else at your school has YouViews. Some of your teachers probably don't even know they exist. You aren't allowed to use your phone at school, so the same rule applies to YouViews."

"Okay, but can I still *wear* them at school?" Bridget liked the way she looked in the glasses. A lot of her friends wore fashion frames like these.

"Okay," Bridget's dad agreed. "But you need to have them turned off, just like your phone. Okay?"

Bridget nodded. Resisting the temptation to use the YouViews at school would be difficult. But she knew she had to follow the rules if she wanted to keep her new gadget.

The next day, Bridget couldn't wait to get to school and show off her YouViews. From just looking at her, no one could have guessed that Bridget's new specs weren't ordinary prescription glasses. Walking the halls, Bridget felt like a secret agent in a movie with a sneaky, hidden gadget.

"Since when do you need glasses?" Bridget's friend Emma asked, walking up to Bridget at her locker that morning.

"I don't," Bridget said with a mischievous grin.

"Oh, fashion frames," Emma said. "You look really cute in them."

"It's better than that," Bridget said. "These aren't ordinary glasses. My dad gave them to me for my birthday. They're from Lingo."

Emma's hazel eyes widened. Then she smiled. "A gadget? Cool!"

"You bet." Bridget told Emma all about the YouViews.

"That's awesome. What does a text look like on those? Can I try?"

Bridget groaned. "I wish. My dad says I can't use them at school."

"That's dumb. It's not like he'd ever find out anyway."

Bridget knew what Emma was thinking. Sometimes Emma and Bridget sneaked text messages to each other during the school day.

"I can't," Bridget explained. "If I got caught my dad would kill me. Plus, they would just get confiscated—same as a cell phone."

"Yeah, I guess that makes sense. But after school, I want to try them. Okay?"

"Sure."

The warning bell rang. They had two minutes to get to first period.

"Ugh," Emma groaned. "Not looking forward to math." Emma had math first. Bridget didn't have it until fifth period. She wished Emma were in her class. It would be much more bearable.

"At least you're doing well in math," Bridget grumbled.

"I mean, I'm not looking forward to it because of the test today," Emma said.

Bridget's stomach dropped.

"What? We have a test? Today?"

"Uh, yeah, on fractions . . . remember?"

Bridget started to panic. In all the excitement of getting a cool new gadget for her birthday, she had completely forgotten about the test. She hadn't even studied, and her math grade was already pretty bad.

Emma put her hand on her friend's shoulder. "You'll do fine."

Bridget sighed. "I doubt it. I haven't studied at all."

"Do it during lunch."

"Yeah, I guess."

"I better get to class." Emma said as she began walking away. "I'll let you know how hard it was at lunch."

"Okay, see you then." Bridget hurried toward her history classroom.

Bridget plopped down at her desk. She wondered how she'd be able to focus through the four periods before her math test. Studying during lunch wasn't going to be enough for this test. Bridget was already pulling a C in math. If she failed, she'd be in the D range, and midterm grades were being posted in three weeks.

Bridget thought about how her dad would react. Up until this year, she had always been great at math. Her dad would proudly hang her graded tests on the refrigerator. But lately Bridget hadn't wanted to show off any of her math tests. She knew that Cs and Bs didn't make it to the fridge. And luckily her dad had been too busy with work recently to ask how she was doing in class. But he'd be sure to see her midterm grade when Mr. Olson posted it online.

Disappointing her dad wasn't the only problem. If her grade dropped again, she'd probably face other consequences. When she'd struggled in science last year, her dad had banned her from using her GameBlast gaming system for two whole weeks so she could focus on studying. He was serious about her grades.

Bridget adjusted her YouViews on the bridge of her nose as her history teacher, Mr. Aster, strode into the room to start class. She'd have to figure something out.

Soon.

Desperation

By lunchtime Bridget was in full
panic mode. She only had a few bites of
her pizza, after she'd soaked up the grease
with a napkin, of course. Bridget flipped
frantically through her math notes on her
tablet computer. They might as well have
been written in Chinese. They made about as
much sense to Bridget.

Emma sat next to Bridget and munched on
some chips.

"You could pretend to be sick and go
home," Emma suggested.

"I can't." Bridget stared at her worthless
notes. "If I did, my dad wouldn't let me play
soccer tonight."

Bridget couldn't let her team down like
that. It was one of the last games of the season.

Bridget rubbed her face with her hands. She looked down at the notes. She imagined her dad seeing her midterm grade and then gathering up all her gadgets, locking them away until she improved her math grade. She couldn't live without her tech!

Bridget knew there was one other way to pass this test. It was a thought she had tried to ignore, but it kept popping back into her head.

She could cheat.

It wouldn't be that hard. Bridget had heard of other kids using their phones to text each other answers. Sometimes they got caught and had their phones taken away. But *sometimes* they got away with it. And cheating would be even easier for Bridget—she had her YouViews.

Bridget didn't really like the idea of cheating, but she felt desperate. She couldn't afford to fail this test.

Before Bridget could say anything, Emma saw it on her face. Best friends were like that.

"I hope you're not thinking . . ."

Bridget shrugged and raised her eyebrows. "It might be the only way," she whispered.

Emma lowered her voice. "What if you get caught?"

Bridget felt a little insulted. Emma didn't think she was capable of cheating without getting caught? It's not like it was rocket science. Plus, with her YouViews, Bridget wasn't an ordinary student—she was secret agent Gadget.

"I won't get caught," Bridget said. "Not with these." Bridget touched the frame of her YouViews. "Teachers don't even know they exist."

Emma shook her head. "I don't know . . ."

"Look, I can't fail this test. I just can't." Bridget was surprised when tears started to form in the corners of her eyes.

Emma's expression changed from stern to sympathetic. She held Bridget's hand.

"It's okay, Gadg. I understand. It's just this once. And, you're right. You won't get caught."

Bridget looked up at the clock on the cafeteria wall. Only ten minutes left before lunch ended. Time was running out. She looked at Emma.

"Does that mean you'll help me?"

3

Making a Deal

Bridget held her breath waiting for Emma to respond. She had less than ten minutes before lunch ended, and then she'd be heading to math class to take the test.

"I took the test more than four hours ago, Gadg," Emma reminded her. "I barely remember the questions, much less the answers. Plus, Mr. Olson changes up the questions for different periods."

Bridget sank in her chair. Who was she going to get to give her the answers?

"What about Trevor?" Emma asked. "Isn't he in your class?"

Bridget looked over at Trevor, who was sitting a few tables away with a bunch of other members from Tech Club. Bridget knew Trevor pretty well because she was in Tech Club too, and he was the club's president. Everyone at school considered Trevor a genius. Especially at math.

"How am I going to convince him to help?" Bridget wondered aloud.

Emma shrugged. "I don't know. But you'd better move fast."

Bridget glanced at the clock. Only five minutes left of lunch hour. In the movies, secret agents sometimes had to defuse bombs as they counted down to the final seconds. She could do this. She had minutes to convince Trevor, an overachieving rule-follower, to help her.

As Trevor got up to return his lunch tray, Bridget saw her opportunity. She leapt from her seat.

"Good luck!" Emma yelled after her. Bridget needed a lot of luck. Trevor wasn't the kind of kid who broke school rules.

Bridget headed Trevor off by the trash cans.

"Hey, Trevor," she began. Bridget's voice shook a little. She didn't know what she'd do if Trevor refused to help.

"Hi, Bridget." Trevor dumped his leftovers into the compost bin.

"Um, can you talk for a minute?"

"Yeah, okay," said Trevor, sounding suspicious.

Bridget scanned the crowds of kids around them. Teachers swarmed the cafeteria, keeping watch.

"Let's go somewhere else." Bridget motioned to the far corner of the cafeteria, near the vending machines.

Trevor made an expression that Bridget recognized as his serious face. It was the same look he had when he argued with her in Tech Club about the best operating systems. She wasn't off to a great start.

"It's about math class," Bridget said quickly. "I just have a question . . . about math."

"Um, okay," Trevor said as he followed Bridget. They were mostly out of sight of the teachers and definitely out of earshot.

"I'm really sorry about this, Trevor. But I've got a huge favor to ask you. And there's only like three minutes left of lunch . . . so I need an answer quick."

"What is it?" Trevor seemed to soften a little when he saw how worried Bridget was.

"I need you to give me the answers to the math test." Bridget blurted out the words quickly before she could lose her nerve. "I didn't get a chance to study. Can you to text them to me during the test?" Bridget showed Trevor her YouViews and explained how she'd use them to read his texts.

Trevor's face lit up. "These are YouViews? I haven't seen them in person yet. So awesome!"

"Will you help me? *Please?* I can't fail this test."

"I'd like to help." Trevor frowned. "But I can't risk it."

This didn't surprise Bridget. Trevor was a straight arrow. Still, there had to be a way to convince him.

The bell rang to end the lunch hour, and everyone started heading to fifth period.

"Really sorry," Trevor said as he turned away.

Bridget grabbed his arm.

"Wait! I'll clean your locker for the rest of the year."

"Look, I wish I could help. I just can't." Trevor shrugged off her grasp.

"I'll do your history homework!" Bridget tried.

Trevor shook his head.

Duh, Bridget thought. Trevor didn't need help with homework. But there had to be *something* he wanted that she could offer.

"Bridget, it'll be fine. Really. It's just one test. I'll see you in class."

"Wait . . ."

Trevor started to walk away.

Then, suddenly, she had it. What did Trevor love more than anything? Technology. He was as obsessed with gadgets as Bridget was.

"I'll let you borrow my YouViews!" Bridget yelled.

Trevor stopped in his tracks. He whirled around.

"Really? You serious?" His eyes lit up in excitement.

Bridget felt so relieved that she almost laughed out loud. "Yes! Yes! You can have them for the whole weekend. How's that sound?"

Trevor squinted at her. "How about the next *three* weekends?"

Bridget swallowed. That was a long time. How would she explain to her dad why she wasn't wearing the YouViews for three weekends in a row? She'd just have to figure something out.

"You'll text me the answers? No take backs once we get to class?" Bridget whispered.

Trevor nodded earnestly.

Bridget took a deep breath. "Deal," she said.

Top Secret Test

"You may begin . . . now," Mr. Olson announced after the math tests were handed out.

Bridget bent down over the packet of paper on her desk, reached up to her YouViews, and switched them on. She tried to look chill, but her face felt hot. While she waited for Trevor to text the answers, she took a stab at a few questions. It was still gibberish to her.

Some teachers patrolled the classroom during tests, walking up and down the aisles between desks looking for cheaters. Lucky for Bridget, Mr. Olson didn't do that. He did have strict rules about cheating, though. Bridget remembered back to the first day of class.

"If I catch you cheating," Mr. Olson had said, "I throw out your test and you get a zero.

No exceptions. No excuses. If you use your cell phone to cheat, it will be confiscated."

When teachers at Blue Lake Junior High confiscated phones, they were held at the office until the student's parent came to pick them up. You also got after-school detention for a whole week.

Bridget squirmed in her seat. What if Trevor chickened out? What if he wasn't careful and got caught? Unfortunately, Trevor sat behind her so she couldn't see whether he was texting. She didn't dare try to look over her shoulder. It might tip Mr. Olson off.

Suddenly, a picture text appeared on the YouViews lens. Trevor had taken a photo of the first five questions on the test and sent it to Bridget. Bridget read the answers.

1. 34

2. 3/5

3. 1/20

4. 1/2

5. A

Her heart pounding, Bridget quickly copied down the answers onto her test, and waited for the next batch.

When Bridget got out of math class, Emma was waiting outside the classroom.

"How'd it go?" Emma whispered as they walked to Bridget's locker together. "Did you go through with it?"

"Yeah, it was good. I mean, it worked."

"You don't think Mr. Olson suspects anything?"

"I don't think so," Bridget said. "I answered a few questions wrong on purpose so that he wouldn't get suspicious. I mean, he knows I'm not *that* good of a math student."

"Wow, I can't believe you got away with it," Emma said. "That was pretty . . . daring."

Bridget smiled to herself. Cheating didn't feel great, but she was sort of proud that she had been clever enough to pull it off. She really was like a secret agent, and she even had the right gadget to fit the role.

But her smile faded when she remembered that she had to turn over her YouViews to Trevor on Friday. How was she going to explain that to her dad?

On Saturday, Bridget slept in. She hoped her dad would be locked in his office working for most of the day. Then he wouldn't notice that she didn't have her YouViews.

Unfortunately, he wasn't in his office that morning. He was reading an e-book on the couch. When he saw her in the kitchen pouring cereal, he put down his tablet reader.

"Hey, Bridg! Wanna try a new Lingo game? It's still in development, but it's a dance one. I know you like those." Bridget had most of the games for GameBlast: YouStar. YouStar had motion-sensing technology for active games that didn't need a handheld controller.

"Yeah, that would be fun."

Good, she thought. Maybe he won't even notice I'm not wearing them.

"Hey, why aren't you wearing the YouViews?"

No such luck.

"Um . . ." Bridget thought quickly. She couldn't tell him that she let someone from school borrow them. He constantly warned her about lending her gadgets to other kids.

"I just . . . wanted to take a break from them. Not used to the extra weight on my nose, I guess." Well, it wasn't the best lie. A real secret agent could probably do better than that, Bridget thought. She studied her father's face, hoping for some sign that he believed her.

29

"Oh yeah, sure," he said.

"I probably shouldn't wear them if we're playing a dance game anyway." Bridget added. She knew her dad was cautious about her breaking gadgets.

"That's true," he said as he booted up the YouStar for her.

Bridget impressed herself. He didn't seem to suspect a thing. Maybe she was better at this than she thought.

But in the pit of her stomach, Bridget also felt a pang of guilt. Here she was, lying to her dad after he'd given her an amazing birthday gift. She couldn't wait until she had her YouViews back for good and could put all of this behind her.

5

A Liar and a Cheat

On Monday, Trevor returned the YouViews to Bridget at her locker. Bridget was relieved that they weren't damaged.

"They are amazing!" Trevor said. "I know they'll be released next month. I've already saved up money to get my own pair."

"Yeah, they're great," Bridget agreed, putting the YouViews back on. "Thanks again for your help."

"No prob," Trevor said. "You'll give them back to me on Friday, right?"

Bridget sighed at the thought of lying to her dad some more.

"Yes."

"Great! See you later." Trevor practically skipped down the hallway.

"Bridget?" Mr. Olson called, pointing at a problem on the whiteboard. "Can you tell me the answer?"

"Uh . . ." Bridget felt her face turning red. She had no idea. Bridget's math class had moved from their unit on fractions to a unit on decimals. Bridget quickly found that decimals were even more confusing than fractions.

"Can anyone help Bridget out?" Mr. Olson asked the class. "Yes, Trevor,"

"Six point five," Trevor said.

"That's correct. Thank you."

Bridget wanted to melt into the floor. No one else in the class seemed to be having trouble with decimals.

"Okay, I need to pass back the tests from last week," Mr. Olson said after a moment.

Bridget felt her body stiffen. She sat up a little straighter.

"Overall, you guys did really well on these."

Bridget held her breath as Mr. Olson handed back her test. She stared at the big red A- on the front of her test packet. This was her highest score all year. She finally had a grade her dad would be proud of. But the pangs in her stomach grew sharper. It wasn't a grade she had earned.

The bell rang, and Bridget stuffed the test into her folder and gathered up her books. When she looked up, Mr. Olson was standing next to her.

"Bridget, I just wanted to congratulate you on your test. I know you were struggling a bit with the fraction unit. But it looks like your studying paid off."

She managed to fake a small smile. "Thanks, Mr. Olson," she mumbled.

"If you're having trouble with decimals, remember, I'm always available to help."

Bridget nodded. But that wasn't an option for her. If she met with Mr. Olson, he would realize that she still knew nothing about fractions. He'd wonder how she did so well on the last test. She'd have to figure out another way to learn the new unit.

"I'm really proud of the progress you've made," Mr. Olson said.

Bridget nodded again, gritting her teeth. Part of her wanted to shout out, "I cheated!" or "Don't be proud of me! I'm a liar!"—anything to dull the guilt she was feeling.

But she didn't.

6

No Other Choice

The next day, Bridget got a sneaky text message from Emma.

UR not going 2 B happy bout this.

Bridget ducked into the bathroom, and texted back, *Bout what?*

Another math test Fri, Emma wrote.

Bridget couldn't believe it. They'd just had a test! She felt paralyzed. She only had a few days to learn *everything* about decimals.

Bridget texted, *Do u get this stuff?*

Decimals? Yea.

Bridget texted, *Can U help me?*

No prob. VidChat 2nite.

Thx! UR the BEST!

Bridget relaxed just a little. She felt lucky she had Emma. Even secret agents needed allies.

That night on VidChat, Emma screen-shared with Bridget so they could work on practice problems together. Bridget used her DigiPen to write on her tablet, trying to solve the problems Emma wrote down for her.

"So, what's the answer?" Emma quizzed Bridget.

"Um . . ." Bridget felt panicky. The answer just wasn't coming to her. "I don't know."

Bridget watched Emma's eyebrows slant downward on the screen.

"Come on, Gadget! You can get this. Just use a little brain power."

"Maybe I only have half a brain," Bridget joked. "That's like point five brain, right?"

"Ha, ha. See, you get decimals, you just need to focus and have confidence, and you'll do fine!"

Bridget did her best to answer the questions and learn from her mistakes. They VidChatted for over an hour before Emma had to go eat dinner.

"You're doing great!" Emma said before she signed off.

Bridget still wasn't feeling sure about herself.

"Sorry, Bridget, that's not the answer we're looking for," Mr. Olson said as he stood at the whiteboard. "Anyone else?"

Embarrassed, Bridget looked around at her classmates. She'd been studying decimals with Emma all week. She thought she understood them, finally. Now it was Thursday, the day before the test. And she was she still getting answers wrong? It was all so nerve wracking.

After class, Bridget trailed behind Trevor. She followed him to his locker. When she tapped him on the shoulder, he spun around, surprised.

"Oh, Bridget, hey," he said, turning back to his locker to grab a textbook. He didn't exactly look happy to see her.

"Hey, look. I hate to do this again . . . but I need your help on the test tomorrow."

"Again?" Trevor looked concerned. "I don't know."

Bridget knew she had to offer Trevor more than a few weekends with her YouViews this time.

"I know. And I hate to ask you. But if you do this . . ." Bridget paused, glancing around to make sure no one was listening. ". . . I'll get you *your own* YouViews."

Trevor couldn't hide his interest. But he looked worried too.

"They aren't selling them until next month."

"I'll just get you a pair early," Bridget said. "My dad has a bunch of them that go to bloggers who write reviews before they come out. It's no problem." Bridget tried to make it sound easy, but in reality she had no idea how she was going to get YouViews for Trevor without her dad knowing.

"Okay," Trevor said. "You've got a deal."

"Tomorrow, just meet me by the flagpole before school."

Trevor nodded. "Can I ask you a question?"

"Yeah, sure," Bridget said.

"Why are you cheating, anyway? You've always been really good at math."

Bridget looked away. "Yeah, well, not anymore."

Bridget hurried off to her next class before Trevor could say anything back. She didn't want to talk to Trevor, the smartest kid in school, about how horrible she was at math.

7

Agent Gadget

When Bridget got home, she was
surprised to see her dad's car in the
driveway. He usually wasn't home until
later in the evening.

Inside, Bridget could hear him rushing
around upstairs. He must have something
going on tonight, Bridget thought. It wasn't
unusual for her dad to have an evening
meeting for Lingo. She'd have to put her plan in
motion before he left.

Bridget froze when she saw a box full of
the packaged YouViews sitting on the kitchen
table. It would be so easy to just grab one for
Trevor. Would her dad even notice?

Just then, her dad came racing down the
stairs. He was wearing his work clothes—black
pants and a blue turtleneck.

"Hey, Bridg! How was school?"

"Fine. What are all these YouViews doing here?" she asked.

"I'm taking them with me tonight," he explained. "We've got a promotional event for the media tonight. I'm giving them to tech bloggers so they can review them."

Bridget almost smiled. This fit perfectly into her plan.

"Well, hey," she said. "The Tech Club at school has a blog. Wouldn't it be great if we could write a review too?"

It was true that the Tech Club had a blog and that they probably could write something about the YouViews, Bridget reasoned. And Trevor was the president of Tech Club. So, it wasn't *exactly* a lie.

"That sounds like a great idea, Bridg. I'll see if I can get a pair for Tech Club. Or maybe they could just use yours."

"Yeah, but . . . the kid writing the article, Trevor, he's pretty clumsy. I don't know if I'd trust him using mine. It'd be best to get him his own pair." Bridget surprised herself with how easily the lie came out. She was getting good at this secret agent stuff.

"Oh, I see," Bridget's dad said distractedly. He was checking his phone, probably getting directions to the promotional event.

Bridget leaned over the box of YouViews. "So, can I take one? For Tech Club, I mean?"

Bridget's dad put his phone in his back pocket and scooped up the box from under Bridget's nose.

"Sorry," he said. "I need all these for tonight. I'll see about getting another one for Tech Club next week."

"But, Dad, we *really* need it this week."

Bridget's dad glanced at the clock. "Sorry, Bridg, that's the best I can do—oh no!" he groaned, looking down at a ketchup stain on his sleeve. "Now I'm really gonna be late." He rushed back upstairs to change his shirt, leaving the box of YouViews on the table.

Bridget stared at the box. She pictured Mr. Olson handing back her decimal test with a big red F on it. "It's weird that you did *so poorly* on this test," he was saying. "Doesn't it seem odd after you did so well last week?"

Before she had a chance to think about the consequences, Bridget reached forward, snatched a package of YouViews, and raced

to her bedroom. Bridget shoved the package under the bed and went back into the kitchen just in time to see her dad lifting the box off the table.

"Love you, sweetie," he said. "There're some leftovers in the fridge. I'll be home around nine."

"Love you too," Bridget said.

As the door shut behind her dad, Bridget exhaled.

Bridget was already in bed when her dad came home later that night. She heard him talking downstairs on his phone, which was surprising because he almost always used e-mail or texting. It must have been something urgent.

"The serial number is 343993," he was saying. "Yeah, I don't know what happened. I did a count before I left the house, and I had all of them."

Bridget realized her dad was talking to someone at Lingo about the YouViews she'd taken. He had noticed one was missing.

It will blow over, Bridget thought to herself. Her dad was president of Lingo. It wasn't like he could really get in trouble for one missing gadget—could he?

Tomorrow, when the test was over, she'd confess that she hadn't been able to wait and had taken the YouView. She'd tell her dad that she had promised them to Tech Club for this week's blog post, and, hopefully, everything would be fine.

8

Undercover

Trevor looked surprised when Bridget
handed him the YouViews at the flagpole
the next morning.

"Wow," he said. "I didn't think you'd be able to pull it off. How'd you get them?"

"You know—my dad," Bridget said.

"Well, thanks," Trevor said. He tucked the YouViews into his backpack.

"Don't use them in math class, though," Bridget said hurriedly. This was getting complicated. "I don't wanna tip Mr. Olson off."

"Good idea. See you in class." Trevor hurried into the building while Bridget felt her phone vibrate in her pocket. It was Emma.

Where R u? Home sick?

Bridget hurried into the school and found Emma waiting at her locker.

"You forget to set your alarm or something?" Emma asked as Bridget opened her locker.

"No, I was . . ." Bridget realized that she didn't know how Emma would feel about her cheating again, especially after all their VidChat tutoring sessions.

"I was meeting up with Trevor quick," Bridget explained. "I had a question about a math problem that might be on the test."

Emma's face fell. Clearly, secret agent skills didn't work as well on best friends.

"You're going to cheat again, aren't you?" Emma whispered. "What about all our studying?"

Bridget sighed. She wished there was a way to explain it to Emma so she'd understand. It was easy for Emma to think the test was no big deal. Emma had an A in math already.

"I don't understand the material," Bridget said. "It's just not easy for me."

Emma looked surprised. "But you've been doing great on your homework."

Bridget shook her head. She thought of her low grade and answering questions wrong in front of the class. Why didn't Emma see how hopeless she was?

"Look," Bridget said more firmly. "I have to do this."

"You can't keep cheating on every single test. You'll get caught."

"No, I won't get caught," Bridget said defensively. "I'm good at this. I'm too sneaky."

"I knew this was going too far," Emma said. "You sound like you're proud of cheating!"

The warning bell rang.

Emma didn't seem to hear it. She was staring at Bridget in a way that made her want to run away. Fast.

"I've gotta go," Bridget mumbled. She didn't want to believe that anything Emma was saying was true.

"Okay," Emma agreed reluctantly. "Be careful."

In math class that afternoon, Bridget found that cheating for a second time wasn't as scary. She was still nervous, but she felt more confident too. She pressed the "on" button on her YouViews and waited for her first text from Trevor. She tried not to think about what Emma had said that morning. Emma didn't understand that Bridget was a techie secret agent—too stealthy to get caught.

Before she received the first answers from Trevor, she heard a voice behind her.

"Trevor, I'll take that cell phone, thank you. And your test as well."

Bridget froze. It was Mr. Olson. She watched, stunned, as he tossed Trevor's test into the trash and carried his cell phone to the front of the room.

Bridget snuck a peek at Trevor. He was red-faced, staring down at his desk in front of him.

Bridget's heart was beating rapidly. She knew her face was turning red too.

She cringed, waiting for Mr. Olson to read the text message Trevor was working on and see who he was sending it to.

9

Coming Clean

Bridget couldn't bear to look up at Mr. Olson as he read the text from Trevor's phone. In just a second, he'd see it was Bridget that Trevor was sending the message to. Bridget's test would go in the trash, and any chance of passing math would be wiped away.

But Mr. Olson didn't read her name aloud, and he didn't come over to take the test from her. Instead, he walked up and down the rows as if looking for another student hiding a cell phone.

Suddenly, it was clear to Bridget what had happened. Trevor must not have addressed the text to anyone yet. She was saved!

But Bridget couldn't ignore that sick, empty feeling in her stomach that now seemed to take over her whole body. She peeked over her shoulder at Trevor. He had his face down on his desk. He doesn't deserve this, she thought.

Bridget realized that if she really were a secret agent, a good one, she'd be committed to helping others—not just herself. She had convinced herself that she was helping Trevor out by getting him YouViews, but really she'd put him in a bad spot. This was her fault.

Bridget got up from her desk, grabbed her test, and brought it to the trash at front of the room.

"Mr. Olson," she said clearly as she watched the test packet flutter into the trash bin, "It was me. Trevor was sending answers to me."

Coming clean was not easy for Bridget. Both she and Trevor admitted to cheating on both tests. They both received a week of detention.

Mr. Olson wasn't happy with Bridget. Bridget's dad was even less happy, especially when he heard that she'd taken the missing pair of YouViews and given them to Trevor.

"You nearly got your friend in a lot of trouble," her dad said. "YouViews have a Locate app, and if I didn't find the pair you took, the IT department at Lingo would have activated the app. The police could have gotten involved, Bridget."

Her secret agent skills had failed her. She never thought about that. And it was bad enough that she had gotten Trevor in trouble with Mr. Olson. If the police had shown up at his doorstep, she would have felt horrible.

Bridget's dad took away her GameBlast for two weeks, and no YouViews for who knew how long.

"Not until you prove that you're ready to use them responsibly," her dad said.

He only let her keep her smartphone so she could reach him in case of emergencies.

The next Monday, Mr. Olson stopped Bridget as she was leaving the classroom after math.

"One moment please, Bridget," Mr. Olson said. Bridget's face reddened as she watched everyone else leave the classroom. Trevor gave her a sympathetic glance as he walked past. Bridget was glad that he didn't seem too mad at her for getting him into this mess.

"I know you have detention," Mr. Olson said to Bridget after everyone was gone. "But I've worked it out with the principal for you to come here after school today instead of the detention room."

"Why?" Bridget asked. Was Mr. Olson going to have her clean the whiteboards? Maybe wash his car?

"You're going to retake the test from Friday."

Bridget just stared at him. "What? I thought I got a zero because I . . . I cheated."

"I will give you 50% of whatever your score is," Mr. Olson said. "It won't be a good grade, but it will be better than a zero."

"But why?" Bridget asked.

"Because it took a lot courage to turn yourself in. Most kids wouldn't dare to do that. Plus, you've been doing well on your homework, so I want you to see what you're capable of doing without cheating."

Bridget frowned. "Okay, but you might be disappointed."

"Let's just try it," Mr. Olson said. "Nothing to lose, right?"

Bridget shrugged. He had a point.

Bridget hurried out of the classroom to find Trevor waiting for her in the hall.

"Are you in more trouble?" Trevor asked.

"No—at least, I don't think so," Bridget said. "Mr. Olson is letting me retake the test."

"Me too," he said. "Only I get just 50% of my score."

"I'm really sorry about all this. I should never have gotten you involved."

Trevor just shrugged. "Yeah, it sucks. But it's not your fault. I made the decision. I just couldn't resist the chance to get my hands on a pair of YouViews before they came out. The grade drop is rough, but Mr. Olson's going to let me do extra credit. Hey, you're not wearing your YouViews!"

"Yeah," Bridget said, "Banned for life. Probably."

"My parents made me put the money I had saved up for a pair into my college fund," Trevor grumbled. "So no YouViews for me either."

"Well, let me know if you wanna meet up to watch something on my plasma TV, because that's about the only tech I've got for the next two weeks."

Trevor smiled. "You got it."

"You got 92%," Mr. Olson commented as he handed Bridget's graded test back to her later that afternoon.

"I . . . I did?" Bridget couldn't believe it.

"Well, it's going to be 46% for your actual score."

Bridget didn't even care. She felt like she could turn cartwheels.

"Did you study a lot?" Mr. Olson asked.

"Well, yeah," Bridget said, thinking of all the problems she'd done with Emma on VidChat. "But I kept getting answers wrong during class. I just assumed . . ."

Mr. Olson smiled. "Now you know that with enough studying and help, you can do well in this class. Confidence is a big part of getting good grades in any subject. And, you know, I'm always here if something doesn't make sense."

Bridget couldn't believe it. She was good at math again.

"Your midterm grade is going to be a D," Mr. Olson explained. "But if you keep studying, and if you come in for help when you need it, you can bring your grade up before the end of the term."

"Thanks," Bridget said. "I promise that next time, I'll ask for help if I need it."

As Bridget walked home that afternoon, she felt relaxed for the first time in weeks. She didn't have to worry about her next lie. And she wanted to get to work on proving to her dad that she was responsible. A good, honest grade on her next math test would probably be a nice way to start, she thought.

Bridget texted Emma, *VidChat math 2nite? Let's get a jump on nxt unit! And, mayB movie w/ Trevor on wkend?*

Emma texted back, *TOTALLY!*

Bridget looked at the text on her phone. She couldn't wait to get her YouViews back, see texts right in front of her eyes, and feel like a secret agent again. She knew that from now on, she'd use her skills for good.

The End

Think About It

1. A person's motivation is his or her reason for doing something. One reason Bridget is motivated to do well on her math test is because she's worried her dad might ban her from using her GameBlast gaming system again. What are your motivations for doing well in school?

2. Think about each of the characters you meet in this story (other than Bridget). Which character do you like the best? Describe him or her. Then talk about his or her role in the story. How did this person influence Bridget?

3. Read another Bridget Gadget story. Compare how she acts in that story compared to what she does in *Techie Cheater.* After reading both stories, does it surprise you that Bridget cheats on her math test? Use examples from both stories to explain your answer.

1. Imagine that you are Emma or Trevor. A classmate asks you to help him or her cheat on an exam. Write down what you would say. What advice would you give? Would you help your classmate cheat or try to help in some other way?

2. Describe your favorite subject in school. What do you enjoy about it? Do you think it will still be your favorite subject in high school? In college? What type of jobs might you be good at if you continue studying this subject?

3. Pretend that you have a pair of YouViews. What sort of things would you use them for? Use your imagination to write a story about a day spent wearing these glasses.

About the Author

Mari Kesselring is a writer and editor of books for young people. She's written on various subjects, including William Shakespeare, Franklin D. Roosevelt, and the attack on Pearl Harbor. She is currently pursuing a Master of Fine Arts in Creative Writing at Hamline University. Like Bridget, Mari enjoys technology and new gadgets. She appreciates how technology provides unlimited access to knowledge and brings people closer together. Mari lives in St. Paul, Minnesota, with her husband and their dog, Lady.

About the Illustrator

Mariano Epelbaum has illustrated books for publishers in the United States, Puerto Rico, Spain, and Argentina. He has also worked as an animator for commercials, television shows, and movies, such as *Pantriste, Micaela,* and *Manuelita.* Mariano was also the art director and character designer for *Underdogs*, an animated movie about foosball. He currently lives in Buenos Aires, Argentina.

More Fun with Bridget Gadget

Cyber Poser

A former classmate, Olivia Bates, reconnects with Bridget on her favorite social networking site. But Bridget's not quite sure she remembers Olivia from way back in first grade. Using some online tricks and a new app that her dad's company designed, Bridget sets out to discover whether Olivia is a real friend or just a cyber poser.

Selfie Sabotage

Between schoolwork and tech club and art club, Bridget has little time for fun. When she does finally decide to relax and go to a movie with a friend, she posts a harmless selfie online. That picture, and the lie it reveals, set the stage for another techie problem for Bridget!

Tuned Out

Bridget's on a long road trip, squished between two of her annoying cousins. So she slips on her high-tech headphones and tunes them out. Problem is, she tunes everything out, including where she's supposed to meet up with everyone while visiting Mount Rushmore. With her phone battery dead, Bridget is left to find another techie way out of trouble.

READ MORE FROM 12-STORY LIBRARY

.